JOE and the DRAGONOSAURUS

BERLIE DOHERTY

Barrington Stoke

First published in 2015 in Great Britain by
Barrington Stoke Ltd
18 Walker Street, Edinburgh, EH3 7LP

www.barringtonstoke.co.uk

This story was first published in a different form in
Ip Dip Sky Blue (Harper Collins, 1990)

Text © 1990 Berlie Doherty
Illustrations © 2015 Becka Moor

A CIP catalogue record for this book is available
from the British Library upon request

ISBN: 978-1-78112-444-4

Printed in China by Leo

This book has dyslexia friendly features

For Erica, Maurice and Baby

Contents

Chapter 1

A Dragonosaurus for a Pet

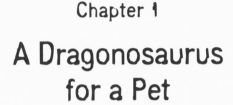

Joe was upset.

That afternoon at school, Mr King had told Joe's class that they were to start a project on pets. First they could tell each other about their pets, and draw them, and make models of them.

Then they could write up charts about the pets' food, care and habits. Later on they could bring them to school.

"What do you think of that?" Mr King asked the class. He sat on the edge of his desk and his teeth flashed white in his long brown beard as he smiled at them.

Joe ducked his head so Mr King couldn't catch his eye. Joe didn't have any pets. His mother suffered from asthma, and anything with fur or feathers made her eyes stream and her breath go thick and squashy.

Mr King could see that Joe was upset. He waited until the other children in the class had started talking to each other in their little groups about their pets and then he came and sat on Joe's table.

"Haven't you got a pet, Joe?" he asked.

Joe shook his head. "They make my mum wheezy," he said.

"Perhaps she'd let you have a goldfish or something like that?" Mr King said.

Joe stared out of the window. He didn't want a goldfish, or a stick insect, or a snake, or any of the other bald pets that people always came up with. His eyes started smarting.

"I'd rather have something big," he whispered. "With a loud voice," he added, as he cleared his throat.

Mr King smiled. "All right," he said. "You can pretend. Pretend you've got the biggest, hairiest, noisiest pet in the class. That's fine, Joe."

Mr King moved on to Lizzie. She was working out a breeding chart for her rabbits.

"I've only got two at the moment," Lizzie said. "But they'll have babies any day now. If they have six babies, and five of them are girls, and they all have six babies, how many would that be?"

"Ten thousand," Joe said.

Then Joe sank his head down onto his desk.

'My pet,' he thought, 'is 12 metres long. With 10 legs. No, 11 legs. And it's

green, and very hairy. And its voice
sounds like metal chains jangling. And
it walks like a big digger. Everything
shakes when it walks.'

Joe giggled. This could be fun!
"The school falls over as it passes," he
whispered to himself. "It gobbles Lizzie
up. And her rabbits. And Mr King, only
I save him. It breathes out fire, and
its eyes light up at night. And when
there's a full moon it flies ... right up,
right up over the village. Its great big

shadow makes all the fields go black.
You can hear its wings ... whoosh ...
whoooosh. And then I call its name –
Dragonosaurus. It comes whooshing
down ... it gets smaller and smaller ... It
lands on my hand, and I snuggle it into
my pocket. It's a secret."

"Well, Joe, have you thought of a
pet?" Mr King asked.

"No," said Joe.

Chapter 2

Fire Clouds

Joe was the first out of school that afternoon.

He put his head down and charged across the playground. His voice rattled like metal chains. The air was so cold that his breath steamed out like fire clouds, and his eyes stung as if they were burning with flames.

He spread out his arms and flapped them till they felt like huge wings. They lifted him up higher and higher over the playground, over the village, over the fields …

"Bye, Joe," Lizzie shouted, as she ran past him. "I'm going to see if my rabbit has had her babies."

Joe gobbled her up.

Joe carried on flying as he ran down
the main street of the village. He roared
at the dogs who barked at him and at
the cats who lay on their backs to have
their tummies tickled.

He flapped his arms at the budgie
in the pub window. As he ran out of
the village and up the lane to his house,
he snorted fire at the nosy horses that
trotted up to the hedge.

Joe charged towards the gate to Rowley's farm and flew over it – the earth shuddered as he landed. He thundered like a bulldozer across the field and roared at a bellowing cow. The more the cow bellowed, the more Joe roared. She kept on bellowing, and so Joe snorted fire at her and made his eyes blaze.

His rattling voice clanged louder than the cow's as he thundered past. Then he stopped.

The cow was bellowing again, with long sad bellows that made her sound in pain, and her eyes rolled.

Joe was scared of cows. They were so big, with their huge swaying bellies, and their voices were so loud and dark. He crept back to her.

"Don't fret," he told her. "It's not a wild dragonosaurus. It's my secret pet."

The cow lowered her head and moaned. Joe felt he would have liked to stroke her, if he'd dared.

Chapter 3

The Feed

Joe's house was just past the other gate at the far end of the field.

When Joe went into the kitchen, his mother was in the low chair feeding his baby sister, Louise. He liked to watch them. It made his mum go calm and dreamy when she had the baby snuggled up to her breast, and it made Joe feel calm too.

"What's this for?" Joe picked up a little bottle from the arm of the chair. It had warm milk in it, and a yellow rubber teat with a hole in it across the top.

"It's a baby's feeding bottle," his mother told him. "Sometimes mothers feed their babies with milk from a bottle. I want to find out what Louise thinks of it. You can have a go if you like."

Joe's mother stood up so Joe could sit in the feeding chair.

Joe sat proud and gentle, while his mother settled Louise in his arms. Then his mum cupped the bottle in her hand and touched the baby's lips with the teat. Louise sucked at it greedily.

Mum laughed. "Louise says it's not bad," she said. "You take it now, Joe."

Joe slid the bottle into his free hand. He bent his head down and saw the baby's mouth working.

As Louise sucked, Joe felt his tongue push up against the roof of his mouth, as if he were sucking too.

"There," Mum said, pleased. "Now if ever I'm ill, or can't get back home in time, you can feed Louise. Whatever else is happening in the world, babies must have their milk."

Mum took Louise back from Joe and put the half-empty bottle down by the sink. "Goodness, she's going to burst with all this milk inside her," she said. "Now, tell me what you did at school today, Joe."

"Pets," Joe said, glum. "And we're going to do pets all term."

"Oh dear." His mum looked sad. "Did you tell Mr King that we can't have any?"

"He said I can make one up," Joe told her. "I've got an 11-legged hairy flying dragonosaurus."

"Lovely!" Mum said. "Now eat your tea and you can go out and play with your dragonosaurus till your dad comes home."

Chapter 4

Spiky Straw

After tea, Joe wandered out into the yard. He wanted to build a den for his dragonosaurus.

Perhaps he could prop some planks up against the wall of the garage and spread some hay under it. There was hay in Mrs Rowley's cowshed.

"You want to be comfy," he whispered to his dragonosaurus. "You don't want to stay in my pocket all the time. You'll want to stretch out."

As Joe rooted round in the shed for pieces of wood and made clanging noises to keep his dragonosaurus company, he heard a long lonely "moo" from the field.

He ran to the gate and peered over. He could just make out the cow, lying on its side in the middle of the field. It was swinging its head from side to side in a helpless sort of way.

"You don't look right to me," Joe said. "You don't sound right."

Joe ran back past his house and up the lane to the farmhouse. He banged on the door. "Mrs Rowley. Mrs Rowley!" he shouted. "One of your cows is badly!"

Mrs Rowley didn't appear. Joe pushed open her door and shouted out her name into the peace of her kitchen. He looked round the yard and saw that her Land Rover was missing.

As he went past the barns he saw a heap of golden spiky straw and pushed a fistful into each of his pockets for his dragonosaurus. He knew that Mrs Rowley wouldn't mind.

The strange noises that the cow was making worried Joe. He'd never heard anything like it before. He went back to the gate to have another look. The cow was still now, and she seemed to be lying back.

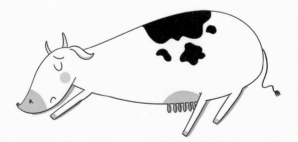

'Maybe she's asleep,' Joe thought.

It was growing dark now, and it was hard to make out shapes, but it seemed to Joe that there was a lump of something by the cow's legs. He climbed over the gate and crept forward.

He didn't want to wake up the cow if she was sleeping at last. But then something moved and he saw what the lump was.

It was a tiny calf. Its hair was matted and wet, and it was shivering.

Joe bent down and looked with wonder at its long, thin legs and its timid eyes.

"Are you just born?" he asked the tiny calf. "Are you all right?"

But Joe knew just from the look of it that the calf wasn't all right, and its sleeping mother was poorly too.

They looked as if they were too weak
to do anything. As if they were too tired
to live, in fact.

Joe stood up and went back to
the farmhouse. Mrs Rowley was still
missing. He had no idea what he should
do.

Joe wandered back to his own house and crawled inside the den he'd made for his dragonosaurus. He pulled out the straw from his pockets and spread it out on the ground, then he crawled out again. The den looked warm and cosy and the pale straw glinted in the growing dark.

"You'll be comfy here," he told the dragonosaurus. Then he sat with his back to the den. He felt odd and hollow inside.

He knew he wasn't bothered about the dragonosaurus any more. He kept thinking about the calf's feeble efforts to lift its head up, and of the cow lying still and silent on her side with her eyes closed. There was nobody to look after them. Only Joe.

Chapter 5

Milk and Blanket

Joe ran into the house.

"Mum!" he shouted. "There's a baby calf, and it's badly."

His mother was upstairs, singing to the baby in the bath. She called down to Joe to stay inside because it was too dark to play outside.

"But the calf ...!" Joe wailed.

His mother started to sing again.

Joe looked round the kitchen for something that might help, and he saw Louise's bottle. It was still half-full of milk. He grabbed it from the counter and pulled her pink cuddly blanket from her pram. Then he ran out again to the field.

It was almost too dark to see anything, but Joe could hear the cow's breath and the light feeble panting of the calf.

He crept up to them and he could see the gleam of their eyes as they turned their heads to look at him. The cow gave a deep moan that scared him. He sat down beside the calf and stroked it. It didn't move at all. The cow watched him with her big sad eyes.

"Here," Joe said. "Whatever's happening in the world, a baby must have its milk."

Joe held the teat of the bottle near the calf's mouth. Its big nostrils twitched a little, but it didn't move. With great care, and a bit scared, Joe prised open its mouth and pressed the teat inside.

At first nothing happened. Then he felt a kind of tug as the calf began to suck. Joe's throat felt tight. He willed the calf to take more milk, making sucking movements himself inside his mouth to spur it on.

After a few weak efforts the calf gave up. It sank its head back, worn out. Joe felt like crying. It was so dark now that he could hardly see the calf at all.

Joe's dad would be home soon, and his mum would be looking for him to go to bed. He wanted to stay with the calf all night, stroking it and feeding it. He wanted it to live.

"Don't give up," he kept whispering to it. "Keep going."

But all the calf did was to give a tiny sigh, as if it was too weak to breathe.

By the time Joe's dad came to the gate to look for him, Joe was stiff with cold.

"Joe, is that you?" his dad called. "What are you doing out there, this time of night?"

"There's this calf, Dad, and this cow," Joe called. "They're poorly."

"Bed," his dad said. "Don't you worry about them. Mrs Rowley will see to them, if they're badly."

"But she's not in her house, Dad. I couldn't find her."

"She won't be far away, Joe. She never leaves her cows for long when the calves are born."

"Can I stop here, Dad?" Joe begged. "Just till she comes?"

"Bed!"

Joe heard his father push open the gate. He leaned over the calf. "Get well! Get well!" he urged it.

Joe put the teat of the bottle back into the calf's mouth and set a stone under it to prop it up. The milk would flow down if only the calf would suck. Then he remembered the blanket. He tucked it round the calf as if the calf were his own baby sister.

The cow rumbled in her sleep. Joe stood up and ran back to his father.

"How's the patient?" his mum asked Joe later, when he was getting into bed.

Joe felt his eyes brimming up.

His mum saw how upset he was. "Don't fret, Joe," she said. "I'll pop a note through Mrs Rowley's door, shall I? She'll know what to do."

But Joe turned away from her and curled up. "It'll be too late," he said.

"Hey," his mum said. "What about your dragonosaurus? You think of that."

Joe put his thumb in his mouth and stared into the darkness.

Chapter 6

More Than You Can Count

Next morning, Joe opened the field gate on the way to school. The cow was still lying there. Mrs Rowley and the local vet were on their knees beside her.

Joe kept his head down and crept across the field by the wall. He didn't want to look at the cow.

When he went out the far gate and turned round to close it, something pink caught his eye. It was Louise's blanket, dragged half way across the field. And standing beside it, on four unsteady legs, was the calf.

It was alive! It was alive!

Joe closed the gate and rushed down to school. He felt as if he were flying, really flying.

Joe couldn't focus on anything that day. All he wanted was to get back home and see if it was really true. Perhaps he'd imagined it.

At the end of the afternoon, Mr King gathered the children round him to talk about their pets.

Joe still felt as if he were far away, on his knees in the cold dark field, listening to the shuddering gasps of the sick calf.

"Who's going to speak first?" Mr King asked.

"Me!" Lizzie said. "My rabbit had her babies! They were born last night. She had 8! And 7 of them are girls, Mr King.

So if they all have 8 babies, I'll have ... erm ..."

"More than you can count, by the sound of it." Mr King laughed. "Come on, Lizzie, try ... Now, how about you, Joe?"

"A billion," Joe said.

"Joe!" Mr King said.

Joe smiled. "Sixty-six, Mr King."

"Let Lizzie do the maths," Mr King said. "I mean, how about your pet?"

Joe tried to remember his dragonosaurus. "It's got 11 legs," he said.

"That's silly," Lizzie told him.

"It's green and it's hairy and it's got a loud clanging voice." Joe put his head down. It didn't sound exciting any more.

"I expect it flies, does it?" Mr King asked.

"That's really stupid," Lizzie said.

"And it eats rabbits," said Joe.

Joe turned away while the others laughed.

He stuffed his fists into his pockets
and let them clench and unclench where
no one could see them. Lizzie was right.
It was a stupid pet.

"Let's hear about Tom's cats then,"
Mr King said. He winked at Joe, but Joe
didn't wink back as he usually would.

Joe took his hand out of his
pocket and opened it out. Now his
dragonosaurus could fly out of the
window. That was the best thing. To set
it free.

Chapter 7

The Land Rover

When Joe came out of school, Mrs Rowley was driving past in her Land Rover. She pulled in by the gate.

"Want a lift up the hill, Joe?" she called.

Joe climbed in next to her. He loved the Land Rover. It smelled of manure and metal, and it rocked over the stony track like a boat at sea.

He liked Mrs Rowley too. She ran her dairy farm on her own, and she was always busy, but she always had time to talk.

"I'm glad I've seen you," Mrs Rowley said. "I wanted to thank you. The Land Rover broke down yesterday and I was stuck miles away from home. I don't know what would have happened if you hadn't been around to look after that calf. Well, I do know, in fact. She would have died."

There was a lump in Joe's throat that wouldn't go away. "Is she going to be all right, then?" he asked.

"I should think so," Mrs Rowley said. "And her mother. We'll just need to fuss over them for a few days."

Mrs Rowley turned the Land Rover down her track and swung it round in front of the barns.

"Come and have a look at them," she said.

Mrs Rowley and Joe jumped down onto the muddy cobbles, and Mrs Rowley shouted the tail-wagging farm dogs out of the way. She led Joe into a dark warm barn that smelled of straw and dung and milk.

The cow was lying in the yellow straw, munching lazily and happily. Her calf was sucking at her teats.

Mrs Rowley looked down at Joe. "I think she's yours, Joe," she said.

"What d'you mean, Mrs Rowley?" Joe asked.

"The calf." Mrs Rowley spoke in a low voice, so as not to startle the animals. "You saved her life, so I should say she's yours."

Joe couldn't take his eyes off the calf's spindly legs and black bony body.

"You can come here when you like, and keep an eye on her," Mrs Rowley said. "Keep her company. And when she's old enough you can have a go at milking her. Would you like that?"

Joe nodded. The cow swayed her big head round to look at him, and bent down to nose her calf.

"She'll have a calf of her own one day," Mrs Rowley said. "You could say you'd be its grandpa!"

Mrs Rowley roared with laughter at the look on Joe's face, and then left him alone in the barn.

Joe sat down in the straw and
watched his calf feed. When at last
she stretched up on her thin legs and
staggered away from her mother's side,
he put out his hands and stroked her.
Her eyes were like wet brown moons in
her white face.

"Moon," he said, as he remembered the dark sky of the night before. "I think I'll call you Moon. That's what your voice sounds like, too. Moon."

Chapter 8

Round and Round

Later that afternoon, Joe's mum heard someone shouting in the field. She ran out with baby Louise in her arms to see what was happening.

She stood by the gate and watched Joe as he ran round and round the field, his arms spread out wide, whooping and cheering as if his lungs would burst if he didn't let all the noise out.

They could hear Joe in the farmhouse, and all down the lane. His voice bounced off the hills, so they could hear him down in the village too.

Mr King smiled as he tidied up his classroom for the next day, and Lizzie grinned in her back yard where she was feeding lettuce leaves to all her rabbits.

Round and round Joe went. Round and round.

Our books are tested
for children and young people by
children and young people.

Thanks to everyone who consulted on
a manuscript for their time and effort in
helping us to make our books better
for our readers.

Have you read all the Little Gems?

New!
COLOUR
Little Gems